ReadZone Books Limited

50 Godfrey Avenue
Twickenham
TW2 7PF
UK

For Dad, and the camper. Love you, Sue

First published in this edition by Evans Brothers Ltd, London in 2010.

Every attempt has been made by the Publisher to secure appropriate permissions for material
reproduced in this book. If there has been any oversight we will be happy to rectify the situation
in future editions or reprints. Written submissions should be made to the Publisher.

British Library Cataloguing in Publication Data (CIP) is available for this title.

Printed and bound in China for Imago

ISBN 978 1 78322 423 4

Visit our website: www.readzonebooks.com

George and the Dragonfly

by Andy Blackford

Illustrated by Sue Mason

George watched a film about
lizards and snakes, and creatures
that slither in rivers and lakes.

He said to his mother, "Do you suppose, for my birthday or Christmas, I could have one of those?"

His mum shook her head.
  "Most certainly not! You wanted a hamster and that's what you've got. It's me who looks after him, gives him his tea...

If you had a python, it's not hard
to see who'd have to feed him —
Daddy and me!"

"If I can't have a snake," said George to his hamster, "or a lizard or something, there's only one answer. I'll go to the jungle and live in the trees with a boa constrictor and six chimpanzees!"

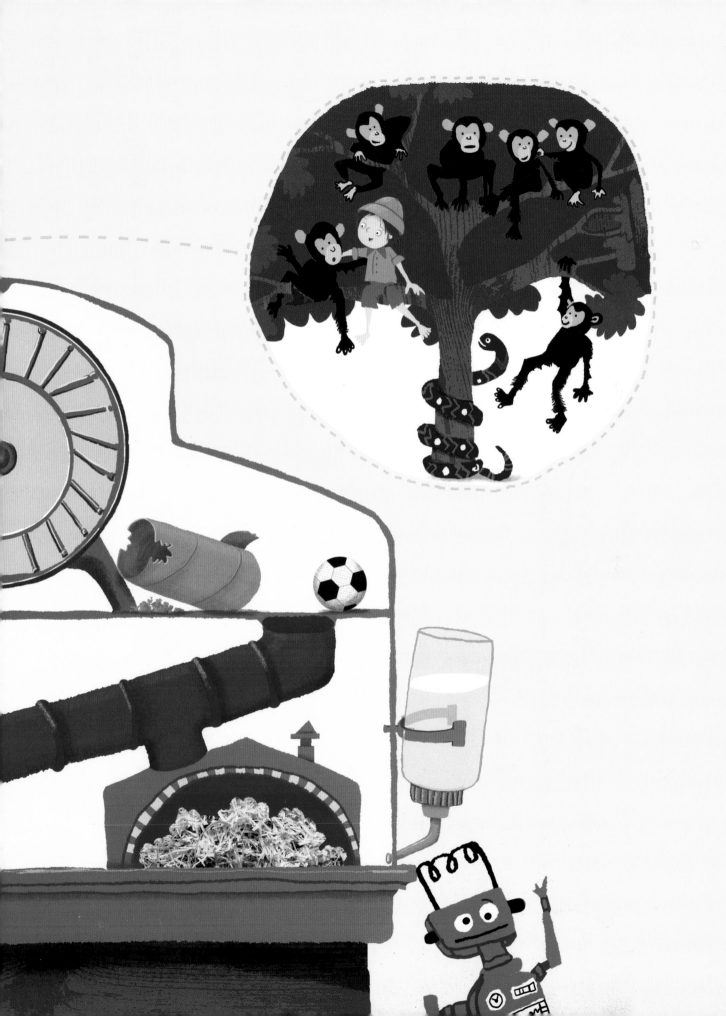

So George packed a bag with some socks and some pants, and left for the Land of Man-Eating Ants.

But George had no sooner set foot in the garden, than a red spotted dragonfly said, "Beg your pardon! Before you go off and live in a tree, there's a couple of friends that I'd like you to see."

George followed the fly to where he was shown. Then, on its instructions, he lifted a stone.

There coiled a millipede, all shiny and black, and a bright orange beetle with stripes on its back.

George was amazed. They were brilliant and pretty — not what you'd expect in the midst of a city.

The dragonfly hovered and darted
beyond, and waited for George by
the side of a pond.

There were tadpoles and toads
and a fat friendly frog, and
a great-crested newt that lived
under a log.

The dragonfly flew to a web on a shrub,
where a red and green spider sat right
at the hub.

Six of its legs were knitting a sweater,
while the two at the back were
writing a letter.

On a twig on a bush, the fly
landed next.
   "I say! Do you mind?" said the twig,
clearly vexed.

"I'm an insect, you know —
I just look like a stick!"
George was impressed.
"That's a brilliant trick!"

"Morning, young George!"
called a big bumble bee.
"Who needs a snake when
there's all this to see?"

But the dragonfly showed him one last surprise — a beautiful grass snake with beady black eyes.

"Thank you!" said George to his dragonfly
guide. "That was totally great."
And then he sighed.

"I think I'll go home and not live in that tree. Why go to the jungle when there's all this to see?"